And to Think That We Thought That We'd Never Be Friends

BY **MARY ANN HOBERMAN**   ILLUSTRATED BY **KEVIN HAWKES**

Dragonfly Books ----✦ New York

All rights reserved. Published in the United States by Dragonfly Books, an imprint of
Random House Children's Books, a division of Random House, Inc., New York. Originally
published in hardcover in the United States by Crown Publishers, an imprint of Random House
Children's Books, a division of Random House, Inc., New York, in 1999.

Dragonfly Books with the colophon is a registered trademark of Random House, Inc.

Visit us on the Web! www.randomhouse.com/kids

Educators and librarians, for a variety of teaching tools, visit us at
www.randomhouse.com/teachers

The Library of Congress has cataloged the hardcover edition of this work as follows:
Hoberman, Mary Ann.
And to think that we thought that we'd never be friends / by Mary Ann Hoberman ;
illustrated by Kevin Hawkes.
    p.   cm.
Summary: A brother and sister learn that friendship is better than fighting
and they soon spread their message all over the world.
ISBN 978-0-517-80068-3 (trade) — ISBN 978-0-517-80070-6 (lib. bdg.)
[1. Friendship—Fiction. 2. Brothers and sisters—Fiction. 3. Stories in rhyme.]
I. Hawkes, Kevin, ill. II. Title.
PZ8.3.H66An 1999
[E]—dc21
98039419

ISBN 978-0-440-41776-7 (pbk.)

MANUFACTURED IN CHINA

14 13 12 11 10 9 8 7

Random House Children's Books supports the First Amendment and celebrates the right to read.

For Munro, Dorothy, and Theo
Thrice blessed
And with homage to Dr. Seuss, whose
And to Think That I Saw It on Mulberry Street
provided both cadence and inspiration
M.A.H.

To the Stephensons—good friends
K.H.

One day we were playing outside in our yard
When my brother got mad and he pushed me so hard
That I pushed him right back—with all of my might—
And quick as a wink we were having a fight!

We thwacked and we whacked and we walloped away,
And we still might be fighting to this very day,
Pinching and punching, my brother and I,
If only our sister had not happened by.

She was sipping some soda pop out of a cup,
And she said she would share it if we would make up;
And since we were thirsty and tired and sore,
We each took a drink and we ended our war.

It's funny how quickly an argument ends . . .

And to

think that we thought that we'd never be friends!

That night after supper we turned on TV,
But we couldn't agree on what show we should see;
I wanted one and my sister another,
And both of us hated the choice of our brother.

And we probably all would be arguing yet
If our dad hadn't come in and turned off the set.
So we put on pajamas, curled up on his bed,
And he read us a wonderful story instead!

It's funny how quickly an argument ends . . .

And to

think that we thought that we'd never be friends!

A day or two later, it wasn't much more,
A great big new family moved in right next door;
How many were in it we couldn't quite tell,
But they each played an instrument—not very well!

One played a tuba and one a bassoon.
They practiced all morning and all afternoon.
They practiced all evening and all through the night,
And they kept us from sleeping, and that wasn't right.

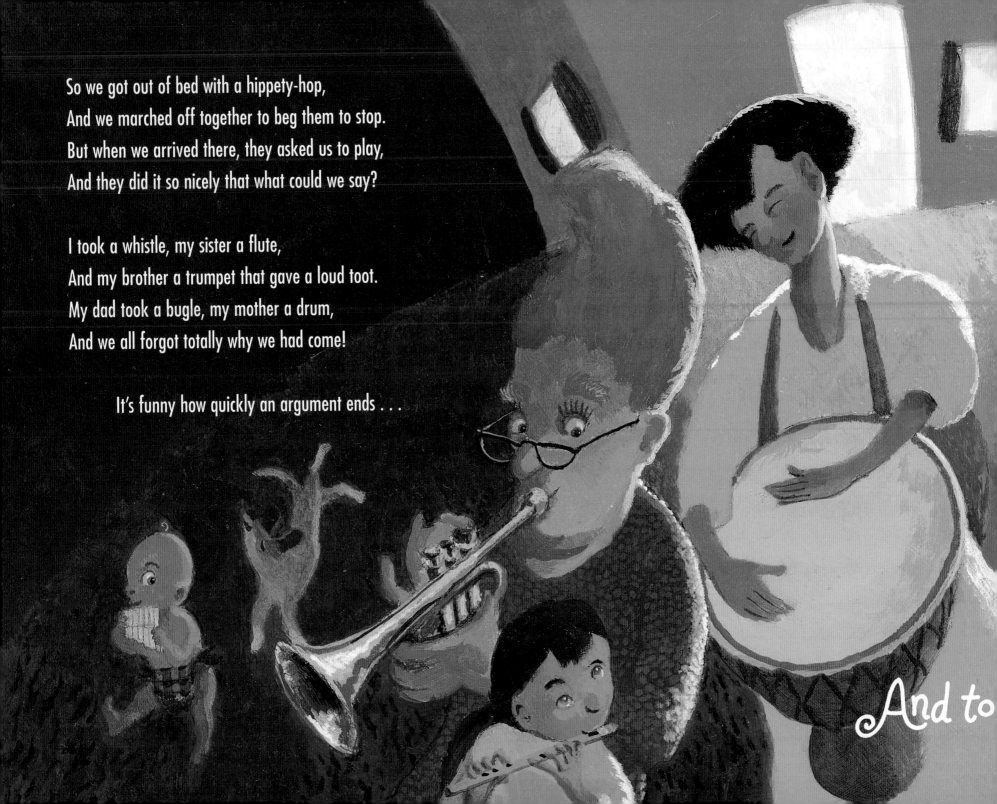

So we got out of bed with a hippety-hop,
And we marched off together to beg them to stop.
But when we arrived there, they asked us to play,
And they did it so nicely that what could we say?

I took a whistle, my sister a flute,
And my brother a trumpet that gave a loud toot.
My dad took a bugle, my mother a drum,
And we all forgot totally why we had come!

It's funny how quickly an argument ends . . .

And to

think that we thought that we'd never be friends!

Then all of a sudden we heard a loud blare
As a siren came wailing from out of thin air!
A police car pulled over, out jumped the police,
And they told us that we were disturbing the peace;

And they said if we didn't stop playing that minute,
They'd take us to jail and put all of us in it!
My brother got red and my sister grew pale,
And everyone trembled at going to jail.

But my mother explained that the noise we had made
Was because we were practicing for a parade;
And she said that the siren had sounded so grand
That she hoped they would ride at the head of our band!

It's funny how quickly an argument ends . . .
Now all of the police had turned into our friends!

We marched down the street, and each person we passed
Loudly complained at our earsplitting blast.
They begged us to deaden our deafening din
Until we invited them all to join in!

We offered them boxes and kettles and spoons,
And once they were playing, they all changed their tunes!
They all were so pleased by the music we made
That they became part of our splendid parade.

More and more people stepped right into place,
More and more people kept up with our pace,
Strutting and striding and stamping their feet,
Marching in time to the drums' steady beat.

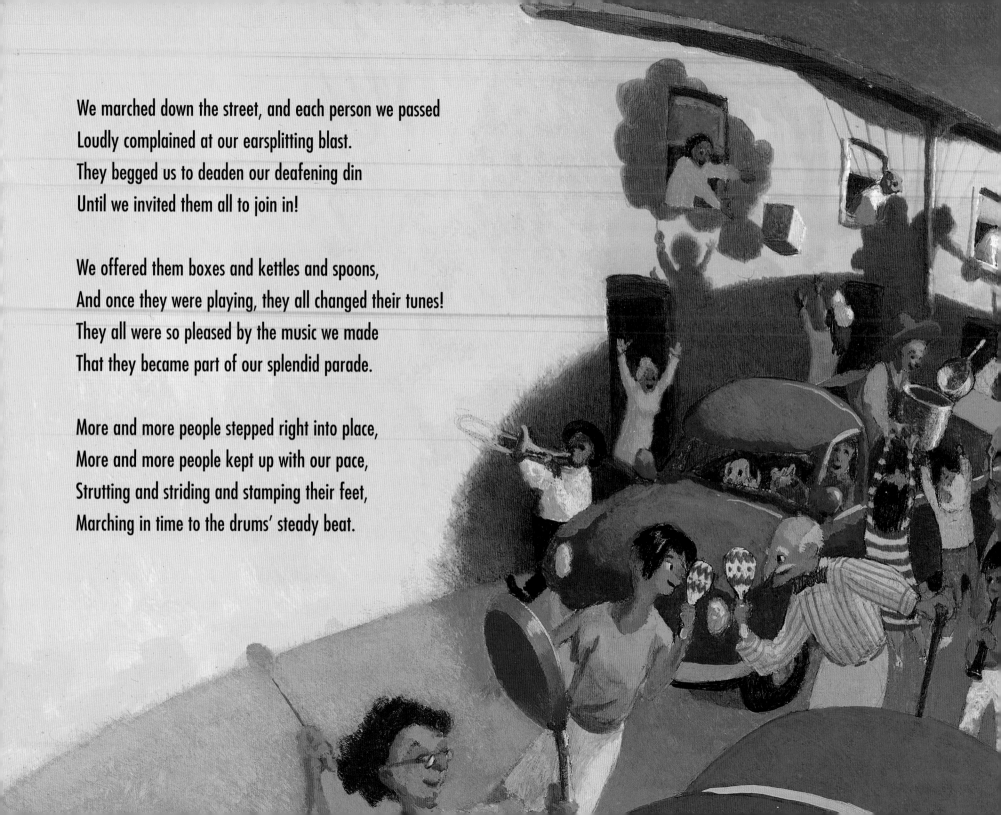

Friends who had squabbled and even stopped talking
Settled their differences once they were walking,
Smiled at each other and marched hand in hand,
Keeping the beat of our wonderful band.

And then we could hardly believe what we saw—
Dog and cat enemies marched paw in paw!
And when our procession arrived at the zoo,
Lions and tigers joined in with us, too!

It's funny how quickly unfriendliness ends . . .

And to think

that we thought they could never be friends!

Our music was magic, a magnet to all,
As to a Pied Piper, they came at its call;
And as we kept marching and tooting and drumming,
The people kept coming and coming and coming!

Hundreds and thousands came running to find us!
Thousands and millions fell in right behind us!
What a cacophony! What a commotion!
Then all of a sudden we got to the ocean.

We came to the place where the whole country ends . . .
With hundreds and thousands and millions of friends!

Oh, what could we do now? We started to fret.
We couldn't keep marching without getting wet.
Then just as we all began turning around,
We heard a most odd and unusual sound.

It wasn't a moan and it wasn't a cry.
It wasn't a groan and it wasn't a sigh.
It was more like a hum humming high up the scale,
A whisper, a whistle, a whimper, a wail.

A wail? No, a *whale!* Yes, a hundred or more!
And all of them swimming straight into the shore,
Singing their whale songs and grinning with glee,
So we jumped on their backs and sailed straight out to sea!

Sharks swam around us while baring their teeth!
Stingrays kept rising from far underneath.
But somehow the songs and the music we played
Convinced them to join in our ocean parade.

For music is magic, it soothes and it mends.

And to think

that we thought that we'd never be friends!

We crossed the wide ocean and washed up on land,
Where people kept hearing the sound of our band.
And even the ones who first came to protest
Soon were parading along with the rest.

And it's hard to believe, but I swear it is true,
By the time we were finished and finally through
And we'd all gotten back to the place we first played,
The whole world was marching in one big parade!

And before we disbanded and each went our way,
We voted to march every year on that day—
To march side by side with the friends we had made
And the friends we'd made up with in one big parade!

And from that day to this that is just what we do,
With the police siren blaring and horns tooting, too,
With our pots and our pans and our trumpets and drums,
And everyone, everyone, *everyone* comes!

And this is our cheer every year when it ends:

Forever and ever,

we'll always be friends!